SINCLAIR, WONDER BEAR

Book Band: Turquoise

Lexile® measure: 560L

First published in Great Britain 2003
This Reading Ladder edition published 2018 by Dean,
an imprint of Egmont UK Limited
The Yellow Building, 1 Nicholas Road, London W11 4AN
Text copyright © Malorie Blackman 2003
Illustrations copyright © Deborah Allwright 2003
The author and illustrator have asserted their moral rights
ISBN 978 1 4052 8203 1
www.egmont.co.uk
A CIP catalogue record for this title is available from the British Library.
Printed in China
70244/001

Egmont takes its responsibility to the planet and its inhabitants very seriously.
We aim to use papers from well-managed forests run by responsible suppliers.

Series consultant: Nikki Gamble

Malorie Blackman ⚡ Deborah Allwright

SINCLAIR, WONDER BEAR

Reading Ladder

For Neil and Lizzy,
with love M.B.

For P.J.
with love D.A.

The moment Emily fell asleep, Sinclair, her teddy bear wriggled out of her tight, squeezy cuddle.

Sleep tight, Em.

He put on his Wonder Bear costume
and set off around the world to see
if anyone needed his help.

HELP!

Is it a bird?

Is it a plane?

He had to work fast. He only had until the morning when Emily woke up to help as many people as he could.

HELP!

No, it's Sinclair, Wonder Bear.

He didn't have long to wait.

'Help! Help! The train tracks are broken and the train is coming!'

Sinclair dived down to land next to a very worried guard who was jumping up and down.

Help! Help! You have to save the train.

'Quick, Sinclair. I need your help. Can you fix the tracks before the train arrives?' asked the guard.

Sinclair could already see the train roaring towards them.

'I can't fix the tracks that quickly, but I'll make sure the train doesn't come off the rails,' said Sinclair.

The elephant's broken the tracks!

Let me see now . . .

And he flew to the tracks and lay down.

'Bear of steel!' he said.

And immediately, he turned into

a bear made of very tough steel -

and just in time too.

I'm as hard as nails.

The train rattled over him, but Sinclair was now made of strong metal and didn't feel a thing.

'Oh, thank you!' said the guard when the train had gone past. 'You saved everyone on that train.'

'Sinclair, Wonder Bear!' said Sinclair.

14

Quick as a flash, he changed from
a bear of steel into Sinclair, Wonder
Bear again. And off he flew, on his
way around the world.

'Oh, help! Someone please help!'
It wasn't long before Sinclair heard
someone else shouting.

Sinclair dived down to see what the problem was.

'Oh, Sinclair! Thank heavens you've come,' said Madame Jolie, pointing to outside her flat.

A lorry had broken down and her front door was completely blocked.

'Lucile, my dog is in there and it's time for her walk,' said Madame Jolie. 'What shall I do? What shall I do?'

'Don't worry, Madame Jolie. I'll handle this,' said Sinclair. He leapt in front of the lorry yelling, 'Bear of magnet!'

And immediately, he became a magnetic bear.

I feel very attractive.

Sinclair was such a strong magnet,

the lorry started to move towards

him at once. And as Sinclair walked

backwards, the lorry rolled forwards

until it was safely away from

Madame Jolie's front door.

19

'Sinclair, Wonder Bear!' said Sinclair,

changing back from a magnet.

'Oh, thank you,' smiled Madame

Jolie, kissing Sinclair. 'You're a star!'

'You're welcome,' said Sinclair. And

off he flew to see if anyone else

needed his help.

Far below him, he could see a big man with a moustache and a tiny woman with a floppy sunhat arguing with Captain Baz.
Sinclair dived down.

Go on, Honey.

Welcome aboard, shipmates.

Arrk!

21

'You said we'd be able to see lots of fish and the coral reef from your boat,' argued the man.

'Mr and Mrs Pincher, you will be able to see them if you look over the side or go swimming in the sea,' Captain Baz tried to explain.

'I want to see them from inside the
boat, not outside,' said Mrs Pincher.
'But that's impossible,' Captain Baz
began miserably.
'I may be able to help,' said Sinclair.

'Come with me and I'll show you how,' said Sinclair. Giving Captain Baz the thumbs up, Sinclair led the way onto the boat.

Quicker than quick, Sinclair removed
a few of the wooden planks at the
bottom of the boat.
Then he lay down to replace
the planks he'd just removed.
'Bear of glass!' he said.

Did you *see* that?

I can't *see*
my toes!

It was amazing! Sinclair was now as see-through as water. Captain Baz set sail whilst Mr and Mrs Pincher stayed inside the boat.

Thanks to Sinclair, they could see the fish and the coral reef beneath them without having to get so much as a toenail wet.

'Sinclair, quick. We need your help,' Captain Baz suddenly called out. Sinclair replaced the planks of wood faster than fast, and everyone rushed to the side of the boat to see what was wrong.

I'm on my way.

'A boy's just fallen into the water.'

Captain Baz pointed to another boat

some way away from them.

'Jack can't swim!' shouted a woman

from the other boat.

'I'll rescue him,' said Sinclair.

'How?' asked Captain Baz. 'You're

still made of glass!'

SINCLAIR, WONDER BEAR!

'Oops!' said Sinclair, looking at
himself. In all the excitement, he'd
forgotten to change back!

'Sinclair, Wonder Bear!' he said
quickly.

'I've got a plan, but I'll need you to hold onto my arm and whatever happens you mustn't let go.'

'What are you going to do?' asked Captain Baz.

'Watch! Bear of rubber!'

And right before their eyes, Sinclair
turned into a rubber bear!

Hold on
tight, Baz.

He stretched and he str-et-ched and he
st-r-et-ch-ed right out, until he could
wrap his other arm around the boy
gasping and splashing in the water.

But the sea spray was making

Sinclair very slippery. Captain Baz

couldn't hold on to him.

TWANG! Sinclair shot into the sea!

Go, Sinclair! Go!

'It's OK, Jack. I've got you,' Sinclair told the boy.

'You've got me?' sputtered Jack. 'But who's got you?'

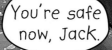

'I'm working on it,' said Sinclair, thinking fast.

Quickly, Sinclair changed into a round lifebelt. Jack slipped the belt over his head and put his arms through so that he could stay afloat.

Captain Baz sailed closer and Mr and Mrs Pincher used a rope to pull Jack and Sinclair out of the water.

'I'm freezing,' said Jack as he sat on the deck, dripping wet and with his teeth chattering like castanets.

'I'll help you,' said Sinclair. 'Bear of wool!'

And instantly, Sinclair was made of warm, dry, fluffy wool. He wrapped himself around Jack whilst Captain Baz and the other boat headed back to shore.

'I'm feeling a bit better now, thanks to you, Sinclair,' smiled Jack.

'I'm glad,' said Sinclair. 'But now I'd better get home before Emily wakes up. Sinclair, Wonder Bear!'

How does he do that?

Sinclair shot up into the sky and headed for home. What a busy few hours he'd had!

Did you see that?

Moo!

41

He flew in through Emily's open

window and snuggled down beside

her. He didn't want to wake her up.

'Emily's bear!' Sinclair whispered.

And immediately, he turned back

into Emily's very own teddy bear.

He yawned a great, big yawn.

'Goodness me, I'm tired.'

And with that, Sinclair fell fast asleep.

And I'm not surprised! Are you?

Hello, me again! Remember the amazing materials I changed into?

Did you know?
Some materials are **made by people** and some are **natural**.

Wool, Wood and Rubber
are natural materials.

Wool comes from sheep. Sheep have a thick coat called a fleece. They are shorn once a year and their fleece is spun into wool.

1 I hate having my hair cut.

2

3

4 It's a lovely warm jumper now.

What things are made from wool?

Socks

Hat

Jumper

Scarf

Rug

Wood comes from trees. Can you think of any other things made from wood?

Here are some other things.

Cricket bat

Guitar

Wooden stool

Cricket stumps

Rubber comes from rubber trees. What things are made from rubber?

My rubber boots keep my feet dry!

Rubber boots

Tyres

Bouncy ball

Steel and Glass are made by people in factories.

Steel is a metal. It is very strong. Can you think of anything made from steel?

Glass is see-through. Another word for see-through is transparent. What is made from glass?

How does it feel?

Ask an adult to help you find these things around your home.

Pick each one up. How would you describe it?

10p coin

2p coin

Metal fork

Elastic band

Button

Paper clip

Drinking straw

Wooden spoon

Pencil

Keys

The magnet test

When I was a magnetic bear I could pull a truck made of steel.

Do you have a magnet in your home?

If you put the magnet close to the materials you've collected, some of them will be pulled towards it. Which ones do you think will be attracted to the magnet?

Magnets attract metals, but not all metals.

2p coin

'Nice to meet you, Mr Alien!'

Mr Alien would like you to introduce himself, but he is very shy!

Is it safe to come out yet?

What you will need:

1 scarf

1 cauliflower

1 carrot

1 piece of toast

1\2 an orange

1 straight face

Ooooh!

It's so poin

1. Cover your friend's eyes with a scarf.

2. First, ask them to pat Mr Alien's head.

3. Then, get them to feel his long nose.

It's rough!

Yuk!

4. Next, stroke his cheek.

5. Be gentle! It's Mr Alien's eye!

How do you think these different things feel?

Can your friend guess what they **really** are?